This book belongs to

ISBN 978-1-4847-8775-5
FAC-038091-17195
Printed in the United States of America
Library of Congress Control Number: 2016936335
First Hardcover Edition, September 2016
10 9 8 7 6 5 4 3 2
For more Disney Press fun, visit www.disneybooks.com

# Do You Want a Hug?

A *Frozen* Book

By Kevin Lewis

Illustrated by Olga T. Mosqueda

Disney PRESS
Los Angeles • New York

Hi, there!

I'm Olaf.

And I love,

love,

love
warm
HUGS!

In fact, I am the

KING

of giving them.

So come on.

Let's hug!

I'm waaaiting.

Maybe I should
come hug
you.

Umph!
Mrfmflm
muffle
mummm

Hmmmmm.
Why didn't that work?

Oh. I get it.

You're playing a game!

If I play a game with you,
will you give me a hug?

# Promise?

What game
should we play?

Leap troll?

Ring-around-the-reindeer?

Wheeeeee!

OH! I KNOW!

HIDE-AND-SEEK!

# HIDE-AND-SEEK!

# HIDE-AND-SEEK!

I'll hide.

You count to ten,

then turn the page.

Done already?

Count again.

BACKWARD this time!

And nooooo peeking!

3 2 1

HE-HE-HE

YOU
FOUND
me!

Now how
about that
HUG!